Dear Parent:

Congratulations! Your child is taking the first steps on an exciting journey. The destination? Independent reading!

STEP INTO READING® will help your child get there. The program offers five steps to reading success. Each step includes fun stories and colorful art. There are also Step into Reading Sticker Books, Step into Reading Math Readers, Step into Reading Phonics Readers, Step into Reading Write-In Readers, and Step into Reading Phonics Boxed Sets—a complete literacy program with something to interest every child.

Learning to Read, Step by Step!

Ready to Read Preschool–Kindergarten
• big type and easy words • rhyme and rhythm • picture clues
For children who know the alphabet and are eager to begin reading.

Reading with Help Preschool–Grade 1
• basic vocabulary • short sentences • simple stories
For children who recognize familiar words and sound out new words with help.

Reading on Your Own Grades 1–3
• engaging characters • easy-to-follow plots • popular topics
For children who are ready to read on their own.

Reading Paragraphs Grades 2–3
• challenging vocabulary • short paragraphs • exciting stories
For newly independent readers who read simple sentences with confidence.

Ready for Chapters Grades 2–4
• chapters • longer paragraphs • full-color art
For children who want to take the plunge into chapter books but still like colorful pictures.

STEP INTO READING® is designed to give every child a successful reading experience. The grade levels are only guides. Children can progress through the steps at their own speed, developing confidence in their reading, no matter what their grade.

Remember, a lifetime love of reading starts with a single step!

Thomas the Tank Engine & Friends™

CREATED BY BRITT ALLCROFT

Based on The Railway Series by The Reverend W Awdry.
© 2014 Gullane (Thomas) LLC.
Thomas the Tank Engine & Friends and Thomas & Friends are trademarks of
Gullane (Thomas) Limited.
HIT and the HIT Entertainment logo are trademarks of HIT Entertainment Limited.
All rights reserved. Published in the United States by Random House Children's Books,
a division of Random House LLC, 1745 Broadway, New York, 10019, and in Canada by Random
House of Canada Limited, Toronto, Penguin Random House Companies.

Step into Reading, Random House, and the Random House colophon are registered trademarks of
Random House LLC.

Visit us on the Web!
StepIntoReading.com
randomhouse.com/kids
www.thomasandfriends.com

Educators and librarians, for a variety of teaching tools, visit us at
RHTeachersLibrarians.com

ISBN 978-0-385-37384-5

Printed in the United States of America
10 9 8 7 6 5 4 3 2

HIT entertainment

Based on The Railway Series
by The Reverend W Awdry

Illustrated by Richard Courtney

Random House 🏠 New York

Stephen is
the oldest engine
on the Island of Sodor.

A long time ago,

Stephen was very fast.

He was called

the Rocket.

SPENCER

Now Stephen is slow.
Spencer calls Stephen
Slow Coach.

One morning,
the Earl of Sodor
gives Stephen
a special job.

Stephen gets to work.

He picks up cookies

from the bakery.

Stephen will be the

Afternoon Tea Expres

He picks up cream
from the dairy.

Stephen likes being the
Afternoon Tea Express!

He gives a happy peep
to Thomas.

Spencer is not happy.

He is behind

the Slow Coach again!

Thomas has an idea!
Thomas gives Stephen
a helpful push.

They go faster.
Stephen is scared
at first!

Thomas pushes Stephen
all the way
to the castle.

The earl is pleased!
Stephen feels like
the Rocket again.

The earl is having
Sir Topham Hatt
and Lady Hatt
for tea.

The earl asks Stephen
to get some jam for tea.
Stephen will be the
Afternoon Tea Express
again!

Stephen collects
all kinds of jam.
He has strawberry,
raspberry,
and apricot.

Spencer wants
the Slow Coach
to move out of his way.

Stephen wishes
Thomas were there.
Thomas would help
Stephen be the Rocket!

Spencer wants to help.
He gives Stephen
a mighty push.
Spencer pushes Stephen
too fast!

Screech!

Stephen puts on

his brakes.

The jam jars break.
Everyone is covered
in jam!

Thomas tells the earl
about his helpful push.

The earl tells Stephen
it is okay to go slow.

Stephen still needs
to get more jam.
The earl and the Hatts
still need to have tea.

Then Thomas has
another idea.
They could all go
for a nice ride!

Stephen may not be
the Rocket anymore.
But he likes being the
Afternoon Tea Express!